SKATEBOARD
IDOL

BY JAKE MADDOX

text by
Brandon Terrell

STONE ARCH BOOKS
a capstone imprint

Jake Maddox JV books are published by Stone Arch Books
A Capstone Imprint
1710 Roe Crest Drive
North Mankato, Minnesota 56003
www.mycapstone.com

Library of Congress Cataloging-in-Publication Data

Maddox, Jake, author.
Skateboard idol / [text] by Brandon Terrell.
    pages cm.—(Jake Maddox. Jake Maddox JV)
Summary: When local skateboarding idol Scottie Devine announces a kind of treasure
hunt in his home town in California, skating friends Griff and Annika are thrilled to
participate—but soon the competition threatens to destroy their friendship.

ISBN 978-1-4965-2631-1 (library binding)
ISBN 978-1-4965-2633-5 (pbk.)
ISBN 978-1-4965-2635-9 (ebook pdf)

1. Skateboarding—Juvenile fiction. 2. Treasure hunt (Game)—Juvenile fiction. 3. Contests—
Juvenile fiction. 4. Competition (Psychology)—Juvenile fiction. 5. Friendship--Juvenile
fiction. [1. Skateboarding—Fiction. 2. Treasure hunt (Game)—Fiction. 3. Contests—Fiction.
4. Competition (Psychology)—Fiction. 5. Friendship--Fiction.] I. Terrell, Brandon, 1978-
author. II. Title.

PZ7.M25643Ske 2016
813.6--dc23
[Fic]
                                        2015035785

Editor: Nate LeBoutillier
Art Director: Russell Griesmer
Designer: Kyle Grenz
Production Specialist: Laura Manthe

Photo Credits:
Shutterstock

Printed and bound in Canada.
009752R

TABLE OF CONTENTS

CHAPTER 1

AN EXCITING ANNOUNCEMENT

Griffin Nash stared up at the clock hanging on the wall in Mr. Barber's English class. Each second that passed was an eternity. Whole species of animals lived and died between the ticks of the second hand. Mountains formed and continents shifted, all during the course of Mr. Barber's lecture.

At least, that was how it felt.

English was the last period of the day. Griff's best friend, Annika Ravi, sat three rows over. She wore the same tortured expression. Their eyes met. Even though they were too far away to whisper, the two friends knew how to read one another's facial expressions.

This is taking forever, Griff said.

Annika rolled her eyes. *Tell me about it.*

Finally — *finally* — the bell rang. Griff slid his notebook into his backpack and shrugged it onto his shoulder. He and Annika navigated through the sea of middle school student elbows, book bags, and feet jamming the halls.

At his locker, Griff snagged his skateboard. It was his pride and joy: blue and white with the sleek lithe form of a blue tiger on the bottom. It was designed by Griff's idol Scottie Devine, one of the world's best professional skaters.

Scottie Devine had also grown up in their hometown of Costa Rosa.

Griff and Annika joined five other skaters at the base of the school's front stone steps. One of the girls, a junior with close-cropped black hair and a constant set of battle bruises, was talking to the others. Her name was Jayne Wilcox.

"No lie," Jayne said. "My sister worked the four to close shift at the Orange Smoothius last night. She totally saw him."

"Saw who?" Annika asked.

Newton, a short but lanky sophomore who looked like a lizard in a pair of blocky black eyeglasses, answered. "Scottie Devine."

Griff's jaw nearly scraped the cement. "No way."

Jayne nodded. "Yep. Dude ordered a Strawberry 'Splosion."

Word on the street was the owners of the town's oldest skatepark, The Depot, were about to make a huge announcement. If Scottie Devine was in town, then he was *totally* the reason.

Griff could hardly contain his excitement. He dropped his deck to the sidewalk and hopped on. "What are we waiting for?" he asked. "We need to head to The Depot. *Stat.*"

"We told Drew we'd wait for him," Newt said.

"Oh." Griff and Drew Coulson didn't exactly get along. Not since Drew *accidentally* cut in front of Griff a couple months back on the half pipe. The road rash Griff had gotten was pretty harsh.

Annika rolled her deck back and forth under one foot. "How about Griff and I just meet you there?"

Jayne nodded. "Cool. Save us a spot."

"Will do." Annika pushed off with her back foot and skated down the sidewalk. Griff followed, his deck's wheels rattling against the pavement.

Costa Rosa was a beautiful California beach city. The sun beat down on the two friends as they rode past storefronts and palm trees and pale tourists hoping to catch some rays. Griff and Annika wove past a family in flip-flops and swimsuits. Griff ollied into the air and performed a flawless 5-0 grind off a bike rack.

"Whoa," he heard one of the young kids say.

The Depot was an actual abandoned train depot and rail yard on the edge of town that had been artfully renovated into a skatepark. Sets of railroad tracks wove around the building. Some of the tracks still had colorful graffiti-tagged boxcars and tanker cars on them.

The Depot's parking lot was full of cars and news reporters driving trucks with large satellite dishes on them. Parked near the skatepark's entrance was a bus the size of a small house. A blue tiger that matched the one on Griff's deck was emblazoned on the side of it.

"It's true!" he shouted. "Scottie Devine *is* here!"

They came to a screeching stop at the door.

"Come on," Griff said eagerly. He stomped down on his deck's tail and flipped it up into his hand. Then he shoved the door open, and he and Annika entered the skatepark.

Griff could hardly move without bumping into someone. He and Annika wedged their way through the massive crowd, past the rental shop and concession area, and back toward the indoor course.

Many of the reporters and skaters crowded around a platform that had been set up next to a wall that featured a brightly-colored mural of a train. Two speakers flanked the platform, and a single microphone stand sat in the middle.

"There's no way Jayne and the gang are gonna see us in all this madness," Annika said. She found a square-foot of space up near the left speaker, grabbed Griff's arm, and pulled him into the opening before it was swallowed up.

They stood like sardines for another ten minutes. As they waited, he heard Jayne call from behind. "Griff! Annika!"

He turned to see the group of skaters moving toward them. Jayne, who didn't really give a rip about other people's well-being, elbowed her way through the crowd.

In the back of the pack, Griff saw Drew Coulson. Drew was a senior, tall and well-built, with a jaw carved from stone. As usual, his expression made him look like he'd accidentally eaten a live cockroach. Which, come to think of it, Griff wished had really happened.

"See that bus out front?" Jayne asked. She stuck her tongue out at a reporter who was frowning in anger at her.

"Yeah," Griff said.

"Told ya that was Scottie slurping a Strawberry 'Splosion."

The crowd hushed. Griff cranked his head to see over the people in front of him. A man and woman had stepped on stage. Griff recognized them as The Depot's owners, Evan and Bryanna O'Brien. Evan had a goatee and wore a short-sleeved checkered shirt and a trilby hat. Bryanna wore a floral dress that showed off her tattoo-laden arms. A thick pink streak swooped through her hair.

Evan spoke into the mic. "Good afternoon," he said. The microphone squelched, then settled. "Thanks for coming out today."

"We love you, E!" Jayne shouted. Many people chuckled, Evan included.

"Hey now!" Bryanna shouted back, jokingly wagging a finger at Jayne.

Evan continued. "First off, I just want to say that we appreciate the years of support you've all given us." The crowd applauded. "I was gonna make this introduction a surprise," he said with a smile, "but I'm guessing you all saw the bus in the parking lot."

Laughs all around.

"So without further ado, I give you Costa Rosa's very own *Scottie Devine*!"

The crowd erupted in cheers. Many of the skaters banged their decks against the floor as an energetic man leaped on stage. He was short and muscular with a buzz cut and a wild beard. His shirt looked like it had been splattered in paint, then smeared into the image of a blue tiger.

"What's up, Costa Rosa?!" Scottie's mellow voice bounced off The Depot's walls. Griff, Annika, and the entire crowd hooted and hollered. Jayne let out another piercing whistle.

"Aw man, it's so good to be home," Scottie said. "This place brings back some killer memories. I was a noob when The Depot opened, and I remember coming here every day. It helped me so much. To be a better student. To work hard. To be the best boarder — *best person* — I could be. And for that, I say thank you!"

Another round of killer applause echoed through the skatepark. Scottie hugged Evan and Bryanna.

"Now," Scottie continued, "to give back to the place that made me who I am, I've got something special up my sleeves. Next month, Blue Tiger Boards — and yours truly, natch — are gonna host an exhibition, right here at The Depot."

Griff was floored. *This day could seriously not get any better!*

Or so he thought.

Scottie Devine wasn't done, though. "Me and my pro skater pals are lined up and ready to rock the half pipe," he said. "But we're looking for three special guests to join us."

The crowd murmured to one another.

"If you follow me on InstaPhoto," Scottie explained, "then you know I like to have fun. Play some games. And this game? Well, it's pretty wicked. Cuz I'm gonna hide three decks—three golden skateboard decks—around Costa Rosa. And whoever finds them . . . drumroll please . . . *gets to skate with us in the exhibition!*"

"No way!" Griff blurted out.

Camera flashes erupted like strobes, and reporters shouted questions at the professional skater. Scottie laughed, clearly enjoying the chaos he'd created.

Griff imagined himself rocking the half-pipe beside Scottie. "I have to find one of those skateboards!" he declared.

"Totally!" Annika shouted.

Behind them, Jayne's whistle of joy nearly burst Griff's eardrum. Newt shook his head in awe. Only Drew Coulson remained stone-faced.

It was another minute before the crowd was hushed again. Scottie and Evan now stood arm in arm.

"Check my InstaPhoto account tomorrow morning for the first clue," Scottie said. "I hope you know your Scottie Devine trivia. Cuz you're gonna need it!"

And like a rock star, Scottie held the microphone out at arm's length and dropped it to the platform with a resounding *thunk*.

CHAPTER 2

THE WAITING GAME

That night, Scottie Devine's announcement was the lead story on the news. It was all over the Internet too, racking up thousands of views in just hours. Everybody was talking about the 'local boy who made it big' coming back home to host an exhibition.

Despite the fact that Scottie had said the first clue would be given in the morning, Griff kept refreshing his InstaPhoto account all night. He ate supper with his parents and kid sister. Refreshed.

Nothing. Played some video games. Refreshed. Nothing. Blazed through his homework. Refreshed. Nothing.

He slept with the phone tucked under his pillow. His bedroom walls were plastered with images of Scottie Devine in action. There was a poster of Scottie completing a backside grab 720 at the X-Games. Another from when he defeated his friend Nick Burke to take first place at the X-Treme Compete Summer Games. And another from the day he launched Blue Tiger Boards, holding the exact design of deck Griff had propped against his nightstand.

The next morning, a slanting beam of sunlight sliced through the bedroom window. Griff was in that sweet spot between asleep and awake when his phone buzzed. It was like a bucket of cold water had been poured over his head. He was instantly alert, sitting bolt upright in bed and wiping the sleep from his eyes. He peered at the screen.

It was just a text from Annika. *NO 1ST CLUE YET. MEET @ DEPOT. 1 HR.*

Griff grumbled, tossed his phone down, and face planted back into his pillow.

It was Saturday, and the smell of eggs and bacon soon filled his room. Lured like a cartoon character to the scent of delicious food, Griff pulled on a Blue Tiger t-shirt and some board shorts and joined his family. His parents were bustling about the kitchen, while his sister sat in her pajamas on the couch watching a kids' nature program.

"See, honey, I told you. Bacon always does the trick," Griff's dad said while manning a sizzling skillet with a pair of tongs.

Griff plucked a piece off a nearby platter, along with a pancake. "Thanks," he said in a muffled voice. "Gotta go." He headed toward the door.

"Where are you off to?" his mom asked.

"The Depot," Griff explained. "First clue is uploaded today."

His mom shook her head. "Leave it to the ego of Scottie Devine to make kids race around and fight one another, just for a chance to meet him."

Griff rolled his eyes. His mom was not a fan. She often suggested he take down the posters on his wall and redecorate his room.

"Mom," he said, chomping down on the bacon. "Chill. I'll be fine."

"And smart," his dad added. "Be smart."

"Smart. Got it."

While his mom watched him with a look of disappointment plastered on her face, Griff snagged his deck. Then he plucked another strip of bacon off the platter, shouldered open the door, and headed off toward the skatepark.

***

The energy inside The Depot was electric enough to power a small town. Skaters rode up and down the outdoor half pipe, and skated wildly inside the set of concrete bowls. It was insane. Hip-hop music pulsed through the skatepark. Its heavy beats pumped through Griff's heart, into his veins.

Griff scanned the crowd for Scottie Devine, but did not see the pro skater anywhere. He did find Annika and Jayne riding the street course. Newt looked on as Annika flipped her deck up and executed a nosegrind along one of the rails. Her moves were fluid, effortless. There were so many reasons that she was Griff's best friend; her sick moves on a skateboard was definitely one of them.

Everywhere Griff looked, he saw people checking their phones. It was like the place was standing at the starting line of a race, waiting for the gun to go off.

Griff joined Newt.

"Sup, Griff?" Jayne shouted, catching air off a ledge before stopping on a dime in front of him.

Annika was right behind her. "Dude, I showed up five minutes before the place was supposed to open, and the line was around the building."

"Crazy," Griff said.

He checked his phone. Nothing.

Griff and his friends made their way outside to the half pipe. Griff stood at the top of the coping, watching the numerous skaters who already occupied the pipe. Their wheels made the wooden ramp rumble like the belly of a hungry beast.

Griff dropped into the pipe, gathering speed as he flew down the transition and back up the other side. He rotated in the air, performing a mute air. His wheels struck the pipe perfectly, and he carved back down.

On his third pass, just after completing a 360, Griff felt the mood in the skatepark shift. He glanced over and saw Annika waving both arms in the air at him.

"Oof!" Griff didn't see the skater before they collided. It felt like Griff had smashed into a brick wall. He bailed, landing hard on the wooden pipe and rolling. The wind had been knocked out of him.

Griff was on his feet instantly, coughing and trying to catch his breath. He saw the other skater sprawled out on the pipe, slowly getting up.

"Aw, man," Griff muttered.

The other skater was Drew Coulson.

Griff approached Drew and offered his hand. "Sorry, dude," he said.

Drew swatted Griff's hand away and got to his feet by himself. "Watch where you're going next time," he grumbled as he scooped up his board and stormed off.

Like he didn't already hate me, Griff thought. *Fuel, meet fire.*

Jayne's whistle cut through the air. "Griff!" she shouted. "It's up!"

Griff looked over and saw her holding up her phone. The screen blazed brightly.

The first clue!

CHAPTER 3

THE FIRST GOLDEN DECK

Griff plucked his board off the cement floor where it had rolled to a stop and ran over to Annika and Jayne. His heart hammered in his chest. Around him, most skatepark attendees were hunched over their phones and electronic devices.

Annika shoved her phone in his face. "Here," she said.

Griff read the InstaPhoto post aloud. "Clue difficulty level: Easy," he said. "Serving up your first golden deck." The photo showed a stained strip

of wood — *a fence maybe?* — alongside a piece of
rusted green metal. The tail of a golden skateboard
peeked out from behind the metal.

"What is that?" Annika squinted, scrutinizing
the image.

Griff was also perplexed. Maybe finding one of
the decks was going to be harder than he thought.

"Serving up your first golden deck," he
whispered.

"Like at a tennis court?" Jayne suggested. "You
serve a tennis ball."

Griff shrugged. "Maybe," he said. "Not really
Scottie's scene, though."

"Check it." Annika nodded at the Depot's exit.
A few people were hurrying out the door. Drew
Coulson was among them. Panic began to bubble in
Griff's stomach, and his hands began to shake.

"Okay, so maybe it's not tennis," Jayne said.
"Did Scottie play any sports other than skating?"

"Baseball," Newt said. "He played outfield."

"And football," Griff chimed in. "But he quit after he went up for a TD catch during a game and landed on his head. Got a concussion. After that, he decided to stick to *safe* sports . . . like skating."

"So he made vids and raised money to enter competitions," Newt finished.

And that was when the light bulb blinked on over Griff's head. "That's it!" His voice echoed through the quiet skatepark. People looked over at him. A few even shuffled closer, clearly hoping to hear the answer to the riddle.

"Nice work, Mr. Subtle," Annika said. She grabbed his arm and led him toward the door. "Explain outside."

When they were outside the Depot, Annika found a spot on one of the abandoned tracks where the trio could talk.

"Spill," she said.

"Served," Griff explained. "What do you serve, other than a tennis ball or volleyball?"

"Food!" said Jayne and Annika at the same time.

"Bingo. Scottie's first job was at the Shrimp Shack, the seafood restaurant down by the beach. He was a waiter there."

They looked at the photo again.

Griff pointed to the rusty green metal. "That's gotta be the dumpster behind the restaurant."

Annika slapped him on the shoulder. "Griff, you're a genius. Let's roll."

The four skaters raced their way through the streets of Costa Rosa. Griff knew exactly where the Shrimp Shack was. He had been there many times, slurping down oysters or munching on sushi and wondering what the place had been like when Scottie Devine had worked there.

"So who gets to claim the deck when we find it?" Annika asked as they headed toward the touristy section of town.

"Let's find it first," Griff answered. "Then we can decide."

In his head, though, he was already holding the deck victoriously. After all, he had been the one to decipher the clue.

It just made sense.

At the next stoplight, the quartet wove around a cluster of pedestrians and ollied into the crosswalk. The beachfront was still a block away. Griff pushed himself to go faster. He carved into a tight turn and rocketed through a narrow alleyway. When he and his friends came out the other side, Griff could see the Pacific Ocean's crisp blue water stretching out beyond the horizon ahead of him. It was a sight he never grew sick of seeing.

There were many stores along the beach. Street performers juggled, performed magic tricks, and painted images of the ocean.

The Shrimp Shack was a gray building down by the sand. It looked like a rundown fishing shack, complete with a large net hanging from the sign. Aside from an older couple eating on the beachside patio, Griff didn't see anyone hanging around the restaurant.

Griff skated to a set of wooden steps that led down to the beach. He leaped into the air, kickflipped, and landed in stride. Annika, Jayne, and Newt landed behind him.

A small fence ran along the back of the restaurant. And, just as Griff had thought, there was a green dumpster. He jumped off his deck and ran the remaining distance to the Shrimp Shack.

"We found it!" he shouted, reaching the dumpster. He dropped to his knees, searching. "We . . . found . . . . "

Nothing.

"Griff?" Annika said from behind him. He continued to search. The stench coming from the dumpster was unsettling. "Griff!" she said louder.

"It's gotta be here," he mumbled, turning over a cardboard box, moving a pallet. There was no sign of the skateboard.

"Griff. Stop."

He was about to yell at her to help him look, but the words caught in his throat when he saw Annika holding out her phone. An image on the screen showed a girl with a wide smile and pigtails holding up a golden skateboard.

The photo was from Scottie Devine's account.

Its caption read simply: *FOUND!*

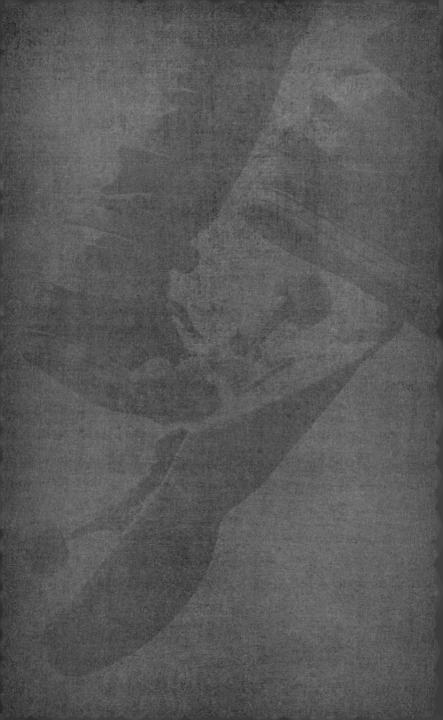

CHAPTER 4

TWO TO GO

The girl's name was Flora Redmond. She lived in a neighboring city named Redwood Falls. Flora was interviewed by all of the Costa Rosa news stations. Griff watched an online clip of one of her interviews with Annika. The two of them sat in his basement on the old couch, eating chips and drinking soda. Griff's laptop rested on the couch between them.

"I just can't believe it," Flora said in the clip. "I'm, like, the biggest Scottie Devine fan."

"Doubtful," Griff mumbled.

"You must be very excited about finding the first golden skateboard," the reporter said.

"Crazy excited," Flora said. "When I searched by the Shrimp Shack dumpster, and actually *saw* it there? OMG. I couldn't *believe* it."

Griff was tired of listening to the interview. He closed the laptop and shoved a handful of chips into his mouth. "I'm finding the next board," he vowed.

It was another six days before the next clue was unveiled. During that time, Griff and his friends skated every afternoon at The Depot. Their usual booth in the concession area was occupied each day by out-of-town guests who'd been streaming into Costa Rosa since the announcement. After the first deck had been found, they filled every vacancy at every hotel. Griff's dad, who managed the Sleep Well Costa Rosa, was exhausted.

Griff had also been dealing with the wrath of Drew Coulson. After their run-in on the pipe, the

Cro-Magnon skater took every chance to harass Griff. He knocked textbooks out of Griff's hands in the halls. He shoved him hard into an open metal locker in the boy's locker room. Once, he kicked Griff's deck out from under him as he rode past on the sidewalk outside the Depot.

Each time, Drew would sneer and say, "Sorry. Accident."

The day of the second clue, Griff and his friends were seated at a picnic table in the outdoor atrium at school. It was lunchtime, and while most of the gang leisurely flipped tricks on their decks or noshed on some lunch, Griff sat with a stack of magazines featuring articles on Scottie Devine.

"I thought you were a walking Wikipedia entry for Scottie," Jayne said before shoveling a veggie burger into her mouth.

"Gotta stay sharp," Griff said.

A gruff laugh erupted from behind him. Drew Coulson stood there. "Man, you're a joke," he said.

Annika elbowed him as she walked past. "Knock it off, Drew," she said. She glared and sat down next to Griff.

"Whatever." Drew grabbed his board and skated away.

Griff watched him leave. "Good riddance," he said.

"Give it time," Jayne said. "Some freshman will narc on him for cheating on a test or something, and you'll be old news."

"Very reassuring," Griff said.

Just then, Griff's phone chirped. He'd set it to notify him whenever a photo was posted by Scottie Devine. More pings and blips sounded around him as Jayne and Annika and Newt's phones all did the same.

Griff snatched up his phone. "Here it is!"

The second image was a burst of green foliage with a hint of gold peeking out of it. The caption read: *CLUE DIFFICULTY LEVEL: MEDIUM. Site of my first bail. Scratched knees and a face full of leaves. Remember: stay in school, kids!*

Griff read the caption again.

Annika said, "It's gotta be his parents' house, right?"

"Yeah," Newt said.

"Makes sense," Jayne added.

Griff wasn't so sure. "Why would that be harder to find than the one at the Shrimp Shack?" he asked. "His childhood home would be the first place to look."

"It's worth a shot," Annika said. "We should scope it out." She checked her watch. "We've got about twenty-five minutes left of lunch. Who's in?"

"Me," Griff said.

"Oh, I wouldn't miss this for the world," Jayne said.

Newt nodded. "Let's ride."

They hopped on their boards and quickly carved through the parking lot and down the street. The four teens wove in and around one another, finding rails to grind and curbs to hop.

Griff knew exactly where the Devine house was located. Scottie's parents still lived there. It was on a small residential block of Costa Rosa, filled with one-story homes and lined with palm trees.

As they rounded the corner, Griff saw a number of people milling around the front yard of the Devine house. He recognized several people from their time at The Depot.

No!

He let up, rolling slowly to a stop in the middle of the road.

"What's up?" Annika asked.

"Drew Coulson," Griff said.

"Where?" Newt peered around, craning his slender neck left and right.

"No. Not here. When Scottie was a kid, there was a bully named Breckin Olsen that wouldn't leave him alone."

"Yeah, sounds like Drew," Annika said.

"He broke Scottie's first deck," Griff continued. "He kicked it out from under Scottie, and then he picked it up and smashed it into pieces on the cement."

"Where?" Jayne asked.

Griff didn't answer. "Come on!" he shouted, turning and cutting across the street, away from the crowd surrounding the Devine house.

I better be right, Griff thought.

There wasn't a single skater in sight as Griff led the crew onto the playground outside of Costa Rosa Elementary School. A handful of kids having recess hung from the monkey bars and soared on the swings.

Griff stomped on his deck's tail. The board dug into the cement, and he came to a stuttering stop. He imagined Scottie Devine as a kid, climbing on his first skateboard, not thinking that a bully was going to break it before the day was out.

And then he saw it. A line of thick shrubs at the edge of the school's parking lot. The bushes looked exactly like the ones in the photo.

"Bingo!"

Griff raced toward the shrubs. He heard Annika shout, "Wait up!" He ignored her.

I'm going to find myself a treasure, he thought with a grin. But as he reached the bushes, Griff's smile vanished and his heart deflated like an old party balloon. A gigantic figure was on the ground and crawling through the shrubs on hands and knees.

Someone was already in the bushes.

The figure burst out like a monster tearing free from its chains, and the hulking Drew Coulson stood in front of Griff. In his hands was a golden skateboard.

"Hey there, loser," Drew said with a sly smirk. "What took you so long?"

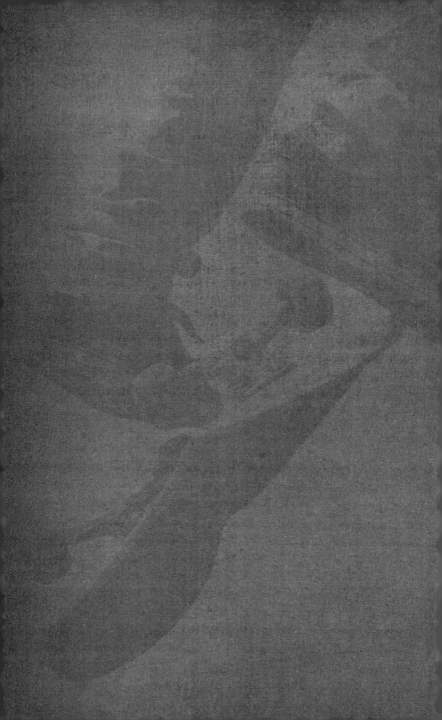

CHAPTER 5

LAST CHANCE

It was like Griff was living inside a nightmare.

Beaten by Drew Coulson? It was embarrassing and frustrating and it made Griff want to shove Drew to the ground and snatch the golden deck out of his meaty hands.

"How did you . . . " Griff couldn't form words. Drew Coulson barely had enough synapses in his brain to fire off during a pop quiz. How did he beat Griff this time?

"Don't cry, noob," Drew said. "There's still one deck out there somewhere." He laughed and waved the golden deck under Griff's nose. "Good luck. I gotta go report this badboy."

Griff stood rooted in place like a heartbroken statue while Drew snapped a pic of himself with the deck and posted it online. He rode off toward The Depot, laughing all the way.

Frustrated, Griff chucked his own stupid board into the bushes. Annika walked over to him, her board tucked under her arm. "Yeah, this sucks," she said, reading Griff's emotion perfectly.

"I almost had it," Griff said.

"*We* almost had it," Annika corrected him.

"Yeah. *We*. That's what I meant."

***

Three nights after Drew Coulson found the second deck, Griff sat with his family eating dinner. It was one of his favorite meals, homemade pizza. Despite her feelings about Scottie Devine, Griff's mom was obviously trying to cheer him up. It fell short, though, and once he'd cleared his plate, Griff went to his bedroom. He flopped down on his bed just as his phone chirped from the nightstand.

It was a text from Annika. *WANNA CHAT?*

He thought about writing back, but decided against it and instead shoved his phone into his pocket.

Griff lay on his bed, looking up at the ceiling. Evening light from the window tinted the room a warm shade of orange. All around him were images of a smiling Scottie Devine. It was like the pro skater was laughing at him.

"I gotta get outta here," he muttered.

Griff's Blue Tiger skateboard sat next to his bed. He grabbed it and headed back out.

Griff didn't tell his parents he was leaving. He also didn't have a destination in mind; he just needed to be on a skateboard. It calmed him down to have wheels beneath his feet. He felt an overwhelming sense of peace with the salty ocean breeze blowing in his face.

Twenty minutes later, he was gliding along the beach walkway. The sun had just dipped behind the horizon, and the sky was a purple and pink bruise. Griff found a set of wooden steps, went airborne, and flipped his deck in a no comply. When he reached the bottom, he picked up his board and strolled along the beach.

He found a quiet spot beside some jagged rocks and sat in the sand. It was still warm from the sun, and it felt nice. The crashing of waves was relaxing.

Griff closed his eyes, took a deep breath —

— And his phone alert went off.

An update.

His eyes popped open, and he scrambled to grab his phone.

A new image had appeared on Scottie's InstaPhoto account. It was the most colorful shot yet, with splashes of bright oranges and yellows and greens. What looked like a swirling, striped blue tail wound through them.

Graffiti, Griff thought.

"Last chance to snag a golden deck," he read aloud. "Clue difficulty level: hard. 'Nothing will ever beat where you first compete.'" Griff shook his head. "That's not hard. Everyone will know that one."

It was common knowledge that Scottie's first major competition took place right at The Depot, back when he was thirteen. He was the youngest to skate, and it had been major news.

Griff stood up and brushed the sand from his shorts and hands. Then he began to skate back down the beachfront walkway, heading toward The Depot.

As he did, his phone buzzed again. This time, it was Annika calling.

"You saw it, right?" she asked before he'd even said hello.

"Yeah," Griff answered. "But it's too easy. I mean, why would he drop the most difficult hint, and make it so simple?"

"Maybe because it's not the right answer."

"Like the fake out with the second clue," Griff said.

"Exactly."

"But if it's not at The Depot, then where is it?"

While the two of them chewed on that question, Griff carved around a corner and through an intersection.

"Wait," Annika said. "Are you on your deck right now?"

"Yeah," Griff said, kick flipping off a curb. "Are you?"

"Leaving now."

Griff sailed down a hill, feeling the clack of his wheels on the cement. He could see The Depot in the distance. The parking lot was full, and there were people milling around outside.

"I didn't recognize the graffiti," Annika said.

"Me either," Griff said. "Except for the striped blue tiger tail."

Grief's eyes followed the train tracks. He could see the line of spray-painted boxcars and tanker cars in the dusky evening light. A number of people were milling around, looking under and around the train cars like a swarm of insects.

"There's a ton of people here," Griff said. He shook his head. "They're all wandering around like zombies."

Annika was silent a moment. Then she whispered, "Sean Fillmore."

The name hit Griff like a ton of bricks. "That's it," he said. "Yeah, yeah. Sean Flipping Fillmore!"

When Scottie Devine was twelve, after Breckin Olsen had broken his first deck, a boy named Sean Fillmore had moved to Costa Rosa. Sean and Scottie became best buds. When the two were just getting into skateboarding, they were very competitive with each other. They'd make wagers and wind up spending entire afternoons skating against one another.

"The deck is under the old Magnolia Street bridge," Annika said.

It's so obvious, Griff thought. *Why didn't I figure that out before Annika?*

"I'm on my way down there," Annika said.

"Yeah." Griff's heart was racing. "Me too."

He stomped on his tail, spun his board, and took off in the other direction.

The Magnolia Street bridge was close. Griff crouched low on his board and focused hard on his speed. Adrenaline coursed through his veins. He tried not to think about how upset he was that Annika had solved the clue.

That deck is mine.

When he saw the bridge and the abandoned parking lot hidden in shadow below it, Griff knew he had the right spot. One support pillar of the bridge was covered in vibrant spray paint.

In the middle of it was a bright blue tiger.

"Annika!" Griff called. He couldn't see her yet.

No answer.

He'd made it there first.

Griff skated to the pillar, then looked left and right. No deck. There was a stack of boxes nearby. He kicked them aside. Nothing.

"Please be here," he whispered. "Please."

And then he saw it, a glimpse of gold flickering in the waning sunset, over by a stack of large, jagged chunks of cement. Griff ran to the stack and grabbed the top piece with both hands. With all his might, he lifted the cement up and shoved it aside. When it hit the ground, it cracked in two.

Hidden beneath it, like a dream come true, was the last golden skateboard.

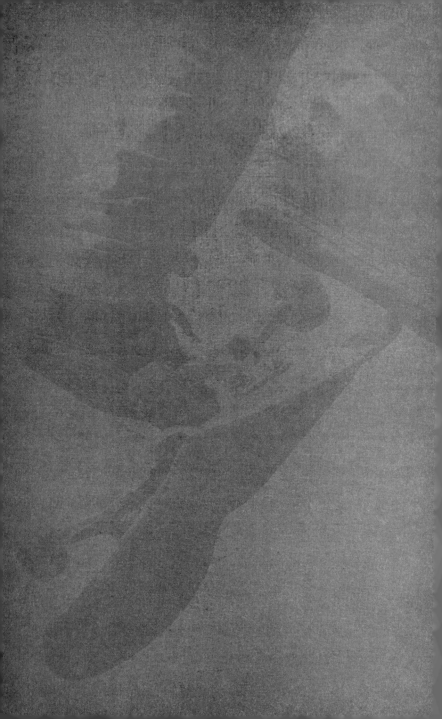

CHAPTER 6

FRACTURED FRIENDSHIP

Griff stared at the deck.

It can't be real, he thought.

He reached out and ran his fingers over the coarse grip tape.

"Yep," he said. "It's real."

Like King Arthur pulling the mythical sword Excalibur from the stone, Griff lifted the golden skateboard from its rocky home. He couldn't wait to show up at The Depot carrying it under his arm. He couldn't wait to meet Scottie. To see the look on

Drew Coulson's face. To skate in the half-pipe with everyone —

"Hey!" Annika's bubbly voice echoed off the hollow bridge underpass. "I was right!"

Griff jumped. He instinctively pressed the skateboard against his chest to protect it.

"We found it!" Annika pumped a fist, then came to a stop right beside Griff. She held out her hands. "Can I see it?"

Griff hesitated.

"Come on, let me see it." Annika reached for it, and Griff pulled away.

"I found it," Griff said.

Annika laughed. "I know. We'll have to, what, toss a coin to see who claims it? Maybe rock-paper-scissors? Or maybe they'll let us *both* skate."

"No way," Griff said. "The deck is mine."

His friend took a step back, furrowed her brow. "What are you talking about, Gollum? I thought we were in this thing together, like always."

"But I was the one who found the board."

Annika's face grew red. "And I was the one who solved the clue."

Griff rarely ever saw her angry; this was one of those times.

Griff didn't back down. "Look, I've been so close to finding the other decks. I mean, stupid Drew Coulson found one before me."

"So you're just gonna claim it?"

"Annika, I — "

"Answer the question!"

Griff said nothing.

"This is *so* unfair. You don't deserve it, Griff. I do."

"No, you don't," Griff said.

Annika walked over. She looked like she was going to snatch the deck out of his hands. Griff twisted sideways, hiding it from her. Instead of grabbing the skateboard, though, Annika shoved him hard with both hands.

Griff stumbled backwards. His heel struck a cement chunk, and he fell onto his back. The wind rushed from his lungs. The deck lay across his chest as he tried to suck in air. Then she hopped on her skateboard, pushed off, and rode away down the street, leaving Griff alone and staring up at the Magnolia Street bridge above him.

***

It was a long, lonely ride back to The Depot. Griff held the deck under one arm. His shoulder was throbbing in pain from his fall. That wasn't the worst of it, though.

Annika was his best friend. Now she was angry with him. Over and over in his head, he heard the sharp words they'd exchaged.

She and I have been friends since before we could stand on a skateboard. She knows I worship Scottie Devine and how important this is to me.

Griff skated by a few people in The Depot's parking lot, on his way in to claim his reward. They whispered as he passed. One shouted out, "Hey, dude! Congrats!" Another said, "Aw, man! Contest's over, folks."

Griff pushed open the skatepark's doors. Two reporters from different news stations thrust their mics toward Griff and asked for a quote. Griff ignored them to search for The Depot's owners.

He spied Evan at the rental counter.

Griff walked up to the owner, set the golden skateboard on the counter, and said, "I believe this belongs to Scottie Devine."

Evan's eyes grew wide. "Wow! That didn't take long at all. You must know your Scottie trivia."

"Sure do," he answered as Annika's words echoed in his head.

Evan held the deck out to Griff. "Guess we better post a snapshot on Scottie's InstaPhoto account and let the world know." He grabbed his phone, pointed it at Griff, and said, "Say cheese!"

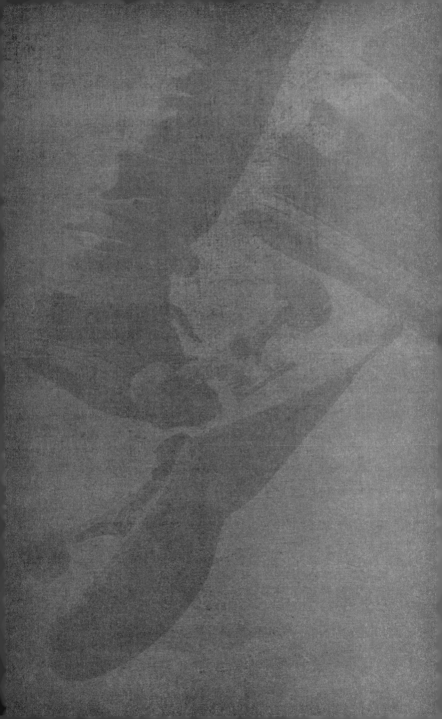

CHAPTER 7

SECRET SKATE

The following day, just past dinner time, a strange email popped up in Griff's inbox. The subject line read: *You're Cordially Invited to Ernie's Pizza!*

Griff was chilling in the living room, watching television with his mom while his dad was upstairs reading to his sister before bedtime. He thumbed open the email and read the message.

For Golden Deck Winners Only! Party at Ernie's Pizza on Seventh Street tonight, 8PM. Back entrance. Bring a friend and your deck. Password is:

Solid Gold. DON'T TELL ANYONE ELSE!! See you there! Scottie D.

Griff fought hard to keep his cool. *I'm invited to a secret party hosted by Scottie Devine? Crazy.*

He was also supposed to bring a friend. Normally, he'd text Annika without a second thought. But since she wasn't talking to him, it was probably a bad idea. He considered Jayne, too, but she was terrible at keeping secrets. By the time they hit Ernie's, half of Costa Rosa would know about the party.

That left Newt.

Griff shot him a text. *SECRET PARTY 2NITE. INVITE ONLY. WANNA GO?*

It didn't take long for Newt to reply with a single letter: *K.*

Griff peeled himself off the couch, grabbed his deck, and said, "I'm gonna go skate."

His mom eyed him up. "Is your homework done?" she asked. The tone of her voice implied she'd rather him do anything other than run off with his skateboard.

"Yeah," Griff answered.

"Well, just . . . remember it's a school night."

"I know."

Newt was waiting for him under the lamp on Third Street, bathed in yellow light.

"So this party's at Ernie's?" Newt said.

"Yep."

"That place has been closed for months, though."

Griff shrugged.

At one time, a couple decades back, Ernie's Pizza was a legendary Costa Rosa hot spot. Even though its classic red and white sign—now rusted and dark — still hung above the red-brick building, the place was boarded up and empty.

Still, that's where Scottie was sending them. So Griff and Newt skated down Third, heading toward downtown.

Ernie's exterior looked the same. Wooden slats covered old, broken windows. Weeds sprouted from the cracked cement by the front door and in between the brick walls. The parking lot was empty.

"Dude, you hear that music?" Newt asked.

He did. And it sounded like it was coming from inside Ernie's.

They rode around to the back of the restaurant, to the kitchen door. A man stood in the shadows by the door.

Griff and Newt nervously approached the door.

"Uh . . . solid gold?" Griff said. His voice cracked.

The man looked them up and down. Then he smiled. "Right on," he said. He grabbed the door handle, and pulled it open.

With their decks tucked under their arms, Griff and Newt entered the defunct pizza joint.

The place was unbelievable. Lights had been strung up along the exposed ceiling, and a giant halfpipe had been constructed in the middle of the hollow space. Skaters were performing an array of moves on it. A punk band was ripping it up in the corner. A group of people watched, swaying and nodding their heads to the beat.

And even though it had been shut down for ages, the place smelled a little like pizza.

Griff saw Scottie Devine chatting with a man with tattoo-sleeved arms and a bald head. Newt shoved Griff in the arm. "Dude! That's Nick Burke!" he shouted.

Burke and Scottie were best friends, but the only time Griff ever saw them, they were competing against each other. It was surreal to watch them talking and laughing with one another.

Griff scanned the party crowd. Ernie's wasn't packed, but there were still a fair amount of people. He spied Flora Redmond with a tall, long-legged skater girl. They were jamming out to the music. A bunch of the crew members were hanging out.

Newt nodded to a booth set up with Blue Tiger Roar energy drinks. "Yo! Let's get something to drink," he suggested.

"Good call." Griff turned and nearly ran into another skater. "Oh. Sorry," he said. Then he looked up, and saw the person he'd almost bowled over.

It was Annika.

"You?!" He didn't mean to say it. Especially not the way he had. He was just surprised to see her.

She didn't take it that way. "Yeah. Great to see you too, Griff."

"Well, if it ain't the lucky loser." Drew Coulson came up from behind Annika, a smug look on his smug face.

Griff didn't know what to say. Sure, he assumed Drew would be at the party. But could it really be true? "You're not . . . you're not here with *him*, are you?" he asked Annika.

She shrugged. "Why not? At least he invited me."

"Come on," Drew said. "The halfpipe traffic is light. We should take a turn."

Cool." She brushed past Griff without another word.

Griff's mood took a nosedive, and suddenly, the party was bumming him out.

"Still want a Roar?" Newt asked, heading toward the energy drink table.

Griff shook his head.

He watched as Drew playfully shoved Annika up toward the pipe's steps. She climbed up, stood atop the coping, and gave a thumbs-up. Then she dropped in.

Annika's grace and agility was apparent as she carved down, wove past another skater, and came up the far side of the pipe. She started easy, with a 180, to gather speed. The next time through, she started to show off. She soared into the air and grabbed her deck to pull off a flawless kickflip Mute Air grab, her favorite move.

Griff looked over and saw Scottie and Nick Burke watching. Their jaws hung open. "Dang!" Scottie shouted. "Girl's got killer moves!"

That's it, Griff said to himself. He was not going to let Annika steal the spotlight.

He shoved past Drew and made his way to the coping. Without hesitating, Griff breathed deep and dropped in.

He rolled down the transition smoothly. He should have been freaked out and nervous that Scottie Devine was watching him skate, but he was too focused on Annika to think about it.

They'd shared a halfpipe before, and knew how to skate around each other. But something was off now. Griff hit the top of the pipe and shot into the air. He completed a 360 and landed back on the pipe perfectly. He whizzed past Annika as she came flying back in the opposite direction. She saw him, and for a millisecond, Griff noticed confusion and anger in her eyes.

The next time he went airborne, he twisted in a backside Judo air, kicking out his front foot and pulling his board back. He was trying to show off, to prove to Scottie that he deserved to be a golden deck winner.

When Griff came down, he was a bit off the mark. He had to curve out to regain his balance. As he did, he saw Annika coming toward him. The two skaters came millimeters from colliding. Their shoulders brushed together, throwing each of their balances off. Griff wobbled, tried to right himself, but was forced to bail. As he turned and struck the transition on his side, he spied Annika falling from her deck, as well. She crumpled to the wooden transition.

The punk music continued. The crowd kept swaying. To Griff, though, the world stood still.

"Whoa!" Scottie said, stepping into the pipe as Griff and Annika slowly rose to their feet. "Is everyone okay?"

"Fine," Annika said angrily, brushing herself off.

Griff nodded. He walked over to his friend and offered his hand. "Annika, I'm sor — "

"Leave me alone," she grumbled, knocking his hand aside and storming off.

"Whoa," Scottie said. "Looks like the party's over for you, dude."

Griff's ears and cheeks burned red. Without saying a word, he grabbed his board and dashed off toward the exit, ignoring Newt's shouts to hold up and wait.

CHAPTER 8

DO THE RIGHT THING

Griff didn't see much of Annika after the party at Ernie's Pizza. He texted her a couple times to apologize but never heard anything back. She wouldn't look at him in Mr. Barber's class, and she'd even coordinated her locker stops for times when she knew he wouldn't be there.

His other friends weren't much better. Jayne heard about what went down at Ernie's and sided with Annika. "You two need to work out your garbage quick," she told Griff during science class. "You're worse than my parents."

Newt still hung with him from time to time, though Griff was pretty sure that was out of obligation, since Griff had taken him to the party at Ernie's.

So I'm down to one friend, Griff thought sarcastically. *And he's only chilling with me out of pity. Awesome.*

Two days before the exhibition, Scottie Devine's behemoth Blue Tiger bus was joined by others as more of Devine's friends rolled into town. Alongside Nick Burke were greats like Grady Calloway, Yolanda Lowe, and Miley Cho. Some of the best skaters in California were in Costa Rosa. Crews were busy preparing for the show, and local media had camped out in hopes of scoring interviews with the A-list talent.

It was an exciting time to be a skateboarder.

That night, Griff couldn't sleep. He tossed and turned. His sheets tangled around his legs. Sweat poured down his forehead and soaked his shirt.

Frustrated, Griff peeled free of the sheets, stood up, and walked around his room. He couldn't stop thinking about Annika, about the hurt he'd seen in her eyes when he refused to give her the skateboard. And the anger after he knocked her off her deck during the skate-off at Ernie's. Their feud was barely a week old, but it felt like an eternity.

"I need to talk to her," he finally said, sitting on his bed and slipping on his pair of Blue Tiger skate shoes. Then he checked his phone and saw that it was 3:34 AM. There was no way he could sneak out. Even if he could, he would freak Annika out if he showed up at her house and woke her up.

Instead, Griff picked up his phone. He started to text but didn't know what to say. And even if he did, he knew he shouldn't be saying it over a text.

Griff threw his phone across the room. It banged against the closet door and landed on a heap of clothes beside it. Then he fell back onto his bed, face buried in a pillow.

A moment later, his tired-looking mom cracked open his door and peered in. "Everything all right?" she asked.

Griff shook his head. "No," he said.

"Oh." His mom wrapped her arms around her chest. "Well, if you're worried about the exhibition—"

"I'm not!" Griff rolled over in bed, away from her. "I don't want to talk about the stupid exhibition. Just . . . leave me alone."

His mom did not react at first. Then, very quietly, she said, "If you think you're going to skate *at all*, I'd reconsider your attitude. Got it?"

"Whatever."

The door quietly closed, and he was alone again. Alone. With no friends. No one to cheer him on at all.

***

The following morning, after getting a grand total of about forty-five minutes of sleep and avoiding his family as they ate a nice, normal breakfast, Griff thought he knew what he had to do. He pulled on a hoodie, grabbed his skateboard and backpack, and was out the door before his parents saw him.

Griff needed to make a pit stop before hitting school. As he pulled up to The Depot, he saw that a crew was already hard at work setting up for the following day's exhibition. They were in the process of moving one of the tagged boxcars over to the park.

Griff tried the front door, but it was locked. He knocked and waited, but no one came. He tried again. "This is stupid," he said, turning around.

A man with thick sideburns and a squinty face, one of the crew members, suddenly banged open the door. "Skatepark's closed 'til ten," he said.

"Oh, no, I just wanna — "

"Shouldn't you be in school, kid?" the guy asked. "Come back this afternoon."

"It's okay, Larry!" a voice called from behind the crewmember. Evan, the skatepark owner, came running over. "This is one of our golden deck winners."

"Gotcha," Larry said. "Sorry."

Larry backed away as Evan slipped past him to take his place. "Griff, right?"

"Yeah."

"What can I do for you?"

***

When Griff showed up at school, his friends were chilling in the atrium. Annika sat with Jayne. They were both reading from a thick textbook, like they were cramming for a test. Newt stared at his phone screen.

The two girls looked up and saw Griff.

"S'up, Griff?" Jayne asked.

Annika slammed her book closed. "I gotta bail." She stood, snatched up her bag and board, and started to walk away.

"Annika, wait!" Griff shouted.

She spun on a heel. "Leave me alone," she said. "It's not enough you steal the golden deck and then humiliate me at Ernie's?"

"I'm sorry," Griff said. "I'm a selfish jerk who doesn't deserve your forgiveness. I see that now. So that's why I went to The Depot this morning and told Evan that you actually solved the clue that led to us finding the golden deck."

Annika froze, her angry retort dying before it escaped her lips. Everyone around them was silent. To Griff, it felt like time had stopped.

Finally, Annika said, "Um, what?"

"I'm not skating in the exhibition tomorrow," Griff repeated. "You are. And you're gonna be awesome."

CHAPTER 9

SHOWTIME!

Griff showed up at the exhibition with Jayne and Newt. He was carefully dressed in jeans, a short-sleeved button-down shirt and tie, and his favorite Blue Tiger skate shoes. He had his deck with him. He wasn't going to need it, but it was his security blanket.

Evan had given Griff three all-access passes, which the trio wore on lanyards around their necks. It felt cool showing the pass to the security guards and getting ushered in.

"I feel like we're in the FBI or something," Jayne said as she flashed her pass again.

Griff had never seen The Depot look so clean. The rails gleamed. The outdoor half-pipe looked un-scuffed and brand-new. A second, identical pipe had been set up next to the first, on the other side of a railroad track.

In the middle of the two pipes was the graffiti-tagged boxcar.

"Sick," Jayne said in a rare moment of awe.

A stage and speakers had been erected near the building. Media crowded around it.

Griff wedged past two reporters and saw Scottie Devine standing on stage. Flora, Drew, and Annika stood beside him. Griff tried to be the bigger person, to not drip with envy over seeing her up there. Tried, but failed. Yeah, he'd done the right thing. Didn't mean it wasn't hard to watch.

Scottie took the mic, much to the delight of the roaring crowd. Jayne's piercing whistle sounded like it had come straight from a steam engine. "Yo yo yo! Let's show my pals here how we say hey in Costa Rosa!"

A handful of skaters emerged from off-stage: Yolanda Lowe with her vibrant purple hair, Grady Calloway sporting his trademark red ball cap with a grim reaper on it, and Miley Cho with her infamous metal grill in her teeth. As each skater was introduced, the crowd noise swelled.

I can't believe they're all here, Griff thought. *And that Annika is up there with them!*

"And how about our very special guests?" Scottie continued. "The three winners of the golden skateboard hunt!"

Griff cheered loudly for his friend. Annika looked over, saw them, and waved.

"Now how's about we do some skating?!" Scottie tossed the mic across to Evan at the stage's edge.

Loud music pulsed through the giant speakers and rattled The Depot walls.

Scottie and the others jogged over to the halfpipe. Annika looked tentative as she strapped on her helmet and grabbed her board. Soon, she stood on the top of the coping next to Scottie. They bumped fists before dropping into the half pipe side by side, like mirror images. They sailed down through the transition and back up the other side of the ramp. As they flew into the air, Scottie twisted his deck in a 360 varial while Annika performed the signature mute air grab she'd displayed at Ernie's.

"Whoa!" Newt shouted. "Show-off!"

The next time they came back up the ramp, Annika turned in a 360 while Scottie did a frontside 540. Griff admired how in-synch the two skaters looked, how easy Annika made it look.

The third pass through the half-pipe was by far the coolest, though. While Annika brought her deck to a complete and sudden halt, grabbing the coping with one hand and executing a handstand, Scottie used his speed to soar high into the blue sky. He sailed off one ramp, over the tagged boxcar while spinning in a backflip. His landing on the second ramp was flawless, eliciting the largest crowd response yet.

"That. Was. *Amazing!*" Griff shouted, raising both fists into the air victoriously.

The exhibition continued with Yolanda and Drew Coulson skating side by side. Griff had to admit, even though Drew was a tool, he looked solid on the halfpipe. He used his speed well, launching himself into a perfect rocket air like it was as easy as ollieing off a curb.

As Griff watched, he clutched his skateboard tighter. It took all his strength not to scurry to the top of the coping and join Annika.

But this was her moment to shine.

CHAPTER 10

DREAM COME TRUE

With the exhibition over and most of the crowd gone, Griff found himself seated at his usual booth inside The Depot. Newt and Jayne were there, as well, noshing on snacks from the concession stand. Snacks they'd *paid* for, despite Newt's attempts to use his all-access pass to score some free food.

"It says 'all-access' on it," Newt said. "That should include access to some chili dogs and extreme nachos, right?"

The concession-stand employee was not swayed.

As they ate, Griff saw Annika enter the park.

She was with Drew, who, for the first time ever, was smiling. It looked . . . *weird.*

"Hey guys!" Annika said.

Jayne leaped from the booth and wrapped her in a big hug. "That was insane!" she said. "You guys killed it out there!"

Newt bumped Drew's fist. "Sick skating, dude."

Griff also congratulated Drew on his performance, eliciting a rare "Thanks," in return.

Then Annika came over and gave Griff a hug. The two friends squeezed each other tightly. "You were fantastic," Griff said.

Annika looked up at him. "That was the most incredible thing I've ever done in my life," she said. "Such a rush." She took his hand, began to pull him toward the door. "Come on, guys," she said. "There's someone who wants to see you."

Annika and Griff burst outside, where the setting sun cast a world of color across the sky. Around them, crewmembers were already hard at work dismantling the soundstage and speakers. People still milled about, talking in groups. Griff saw Evan and Bryanna O'Brien speaking with a reporter for the Costa Rosa Channel 11 News.

Over by the halfpipe, Griff saw Scottie Devine and Grady Calloway.

Annika was heading right toward them.

When Scottie saw them, he waved them over. "Annika!" he shouted. "Drew! Are these your friends? Cool!"

Scottie was still amped up from a day of skating. He was a ball of energy, frenetic and wild. Griff's heart played his ribs like a xylophone as they approached his idol. "What's up?!" Scottie shouted. Then he bumped fists with all of them.

"Hey, you're the kid from Ernie's," Scottie said when he reached Griff. Griff tried to not to look too embarrassed. Scottie pointed at the Blue Tiger board in Griff's hand. "Great taste, dude."

Griff's ears burned red. "Thanks."

"Want to see what kind of killer moves it can do?"

"That'd be awesome."

"Then what are we waiting for?"

Scottie grabbed his board and led the group over to the half pipe. Griff climbed to the top and stood on the coping. Scottie came over and stood next to him. The feeling was beyond surreal. All of the posters in his room and the magazines and the Blue Tiger gear . . . and now here he was. Standing next to his idol, about to skate with him.

Scottie nodded to the half pipe. "Drop in, Griff."

Griff looked over at Annika, who winked and said, "Go big or go home, right?"

Griff balanced on his deck, the nose of his board suspended in midair. Then, he shifted his weight, and was off.

He moved down the transition quickly, gaining speed and momentum. After a couple of passes, he finally felt confident enough to try a move. As he sailed off the pipe, Griff performed one of his favorite moves, a stalefish. When he landed it, the feeling was almost euphoric.

"Woo!" Annika shouted. "You rock, Griff!"

Griff came back up the transition. He popped onto the coping and landed next to Scottie on the plateau once more.

Scottie nodded his head. "Impressive, dude," he said. "I heard what you did for Annika, how you came clean. That's what friends do, ain't it? Solid, man." He and Griff bumped fists. "Mind if I join?"

"Not at all," said Griff.

"All right," said Scottie. "We ride on three."

Griff took a second to live in this moment, to enjoy it and remember it. Because this moment was something he'd talk about for the rest of his life.

Scottie nodded. Then he and Griff counted down together.

"Three . . . two . . . one . . . *GO!*"

ABOUT THE AUTHOR

Brandon Terrell is the author of numerous children's books, including several volumes in both the *Tony Hawk 900 Revolutions* series and the *Tony Hawk Live 2 Skate* series. He has also written the first four titles from the *Sports Illustrated Kids Time Machine Magazine* set, due for publication in 2016. When not hunched over his laptop, Brandon enjoys watching movies and television, reading, watching (and playing!) baseball, and spending time with his wife and two children in Minnesota.

GLOSSARY

deck (DEK)—the flat, long, usually wooden part of the skateboard that a rider stands on

half pipe (HAF PIPE)—a curved structure with high sides that is used for doing tricks

noob (NOOB)—a person who is inexperienced in a particular activity

exhibition (ex-uh-BISH-uhn)—a public showing

coping (COHP-ing)—any grindable or slidable edge attached to an obstacle, like the top edge of a half-pipe

ollie (AH-lee)—maneuver in which the skater kicks the tail of the board down while jumping in order to make the board pop into the air

grip tape (GRIP TAPE)—the gritty, papery layer that's applied to the top of a skateboard deck so that a skater's shoes don't slip

tagged (TAGGED)—a signature or symbol written as graffiti with spray paint

DISCUSSION QUESTIONS

1. Early on in the story, Griff shows his excitement for his skating idol, Scottie Devine. Why do you think Griff is so into Scottie, and do you think Scottie is a positive role model?

2. When Griff finds the last golden deck, it initially makes his life worse, not better. Why does it happen so often that the more "things" people acquire, the more difficult their lives become? Has this ever happened to you?

3. Griff eventually gives Annika credit for finding the last golden deck, and this makes it so that Annika, instead of Griff, gets to skate in the exhibition with Scottie Devine. What did Griff lose by making this move? What did he gain?

WRITING PROMPTS

1. *Skateboard Idol* is largely about Griff's fascination with his idol, Scottie Devine. Write a short poem of 8–12 lines about a person you've idolized. Title your poem "Idols Rock."

2. If there was a soundtrack for this story, what would it sound like? Make a 10–15 song playlist for *Skateboard Idol*.

3. The search for the golden decks is an exciting element in *Skateboard Idol*. Write a one-page essay about a time you or one of your friends discovered something cool.

SKATE FACTS

- Skateboards date back to the turn of the 20th century! The first boards were made out of milk crates nailed to a wooden base.

- In 1959, the 'Roller Derby Skateboard' became the first skateboard sold to the general public. Its wheels were made out of clay.

- California was the birthplace of skateboarding. The sport was created by surfers who created a 'sidewalk surfboard' with wheels. Hang ten!

- In the early 1970s, a man named Frank Nasworthy added a substance called polyurethane to skateboard wheels. This made them sleeker, faster, and made for a less bumpy ride.

- The first outdoor skatepark was built in Florida back in 1976.

- Alan Ollie Gelfand will go down in history as the first person to create a modern skateboarding trick. The 'ollie' is one of the basic tricks every skateboarder learns.

KILLER MOVES

5-0 Grind — The nose of the skateboard is in the air, and only the back trucks grind on a ledge or rail. It's a pretty advanced trick, but it looks awesome!

Frontside Nosegrind — It takes great balance to pull off a nosegrind. Stay over the front of your board and grind on the front truck and nose of the deck.

Kickflip — Ollie into the air and lift your back foot from the board. Use your front foot to 'flick' the deck, spinning it in a 360 in mid-air before landing!

Mute Air — After launching into the air from a half-pipe, grab the toe side of the board with your front hand and turn to your backside to land. Congrats! You've just completed a mute air!

Rocket Air — Blast off by grabbing the nose of the skateboard with both hands at the same time and placing both feet on the deck's tail.

Stalefish — After catching air, reach your back hand around your back leg to grab the heel-side of your deck. It was invented by skateboarding legend Tony Hawk at camp. When he called the canned fish at dinner that night "stale," a fellow camper thought he was naming a new trick!